THE OTHER GIRL

THE OTHER GIRL
ANNIE ERNAUX

Translated by Alison L. Strayer

SEVEN STORIES PRESS
New York · Oakland

Copyright © Editions Robert Laffont, 2011
English translation © Alison L. Strayer, 2025

Originally published in French as *L'autre fille* (NiL Éditions, 2011).

Photos © Annie Ernaux. All rights reserved.

All rights reserved. No part of this book may be reproduced, stored in a retrieval system, or transmitted in any form, by any means, including mechanical, electronic, photocopying, recording, or otherwise, without the prior written permission of the publisher.

Seven Stories Press
140 Watts Street
New York, NY 10013
www.sevenstories.com

Library of Congress Cataloging-in-Publication Data is on file.

ISBN: 978-1-64421-487-9 (paperback)
ISBN: 978-1-64421-490-9 (ebook)

College professors and high school and middle school teachers may order free examination copies of Seven Stories Press titles. Visit https://www.sevenstories.com/pg/resources-academics or email academic@sevenstories.com.

Printed in Canada

9 8 7 6 5 4 3 2 1

Children are cursed with believing.
FLANNERY O'CONNOR

It is a sepia photo, oval-shaped, glued inside a yellowed cardboard folder, showing a baby posed in three-quarter profile on a heap of scalloped cushions. The infant wears an embroidered nightdress with a single, wide strap to which a large bow is attached, just behind the shoulder, like a big flower or the wings of a giant butterfly. The body is long and not very fleshy. The legs are parted and stretch out toward the edge of the table. Under the brown hair, swept up in a big curl over the protuberant forehead, the eyes are wide and staring with an almost devouring intensity. The arms, open like those of a baby doll, seem to be flailing, as if she were about to leap from the table. Below the photo, the signature of the photographer (M. Ridel, Lillebonne), whose intertwined initials also appear in the upper left-hand corner of the front cover, which is heavily soiled and coming unglued.

When I was little, I believed—I must have been told—that the baby was me. It isn't me, it's you.

There was another photo, taken by the same photographer, of me on the same table with my brown hair pulled up in the same sort of roll, but I appear to be plump, with deep-set eyes in a round chubby face, my hand between my thighs. I don't remember ever being puzzled by the—obvious—differences between the two photos.

Around All Saints' Day, I go to the cemetery in Yvetot to lay flowers on the two graves, the parents' grave and yours. From one year to the next, I forget where they are but find my bearings with the tall and very white cross that can be seen from the central pathway and which looms over your grave, right next to theirs. I place a potted chrysanthemum of a different color on each grave, or sometimes a pot of heather on yours, working it into the patch of gravel put there for that purpose at the foot of the tombstone.

I don't know if people spend much time thinking in front of graves. I linger for a moment before my parents' grave. It's as if I'm saying, "Here I am," and showing them what has become of me in the past year, what I've done, written, hoped to write. Then I move on to yours, to the right. I look at the headstone and read the inscription in big, too-shiny gilded letters, crudely repainted in the nineties over the old ones, which were smaller and had become illegible. The marble mason took it upon himself to remove half of the original inscription, leaving a single entry under your first and last name, certainly because he considered it to be of utmost importance: "Died on Holy Thursday, 1938." That is what struck me too the first time I saw your grave. Like proof carved in stone of your being chosen by God, of your saintliness. In the twenty-five years I've been visiting the graves, I've never had anything to say to you.

According to the civil registry, you're my sister. You have the same surname as me—Duchesne, my "maiden name." We are listed one after the other in the parents' family record book, almost in tatters, under the heading "Births and Deaths of Children of the Marriage." You are above, with two stamps from the Mairie of Lillebonne (Seine-Inférieure), I am below with only one. The box for death will be filled out for me in another record book that attests to my reproduction of a family, under another name.

But you're not my sister, you never were. We did not play, eat, or sleep together. I never touched you, or kissed you. I don't know the color of your eyes. I've never seen you. You have no body, you have no voice. You're just a flat image in a few black-and-white photos. I have no memory of you. You'd already been dead for two and a half years when I was born. You are the child of heaven, the invisible little girl that no one ever talked about, the absent one in every conversation. The secret.

You have always been dead. You entered my life dead the summer I turned ten. You were born and died in a story, like Bonnie, Scarlett and Rhett's little girl in *Gone with the Wind*.

The scene of the story unfolds in the summer of 1950, the last great summer of playing from morning to night with cousins, local girls, and a few city girls on holiday in Yvetot. We played shopkeeper with grown-ups as our customers and built houses out of bottle crates, cardboard boxes, and old fabric in the many outbuildings behind my parents' café-grocery. Standing on the swing, we took turns singing *Il fait bon chez vous Maître Pierre* and *Ma guêpière et mes longs jupons*, the way people did in talent search shows on the radio. We escaped to pick blackberries. The company of boys was forbidden by my parents on the grounds that boys preferred rough games. In the evening, we went our separate ways, covered in dirt from head to toe. I washed my arms and legs, happy to know that we'd do it all again the following day. The year after, the girls will have scattered, or fallen out, and I'll be bored and do nothing but read.

I would like to go on describing those holidays, in order to postpone. To tell the story of the story means putting an end to the blur of the past, like developing a roll of film that has been in a cupboard for sixty years and never printed.

It is Sunday, in the late afternoon, at the foot of the narrow lane that runs behind my parents' café-grocery (the rue de l'École, named after a private nursery school said to have stood there at the turn of the century), near the rose and dahlia garden protected by a high iron-mesh fence that runs along the wall over a bank of weeds. On the other side is a tall, thick hedge. For an indeterminate time, my mother has been standing there, deep in conversation with a young woman from Le Havre who is spending the holidays with her four-year-old daughter at the home of her in-laws, M. and Mme S., who live about ten meters further down the rue de l'École. My mother has probably left the shop, which never closes at this time of year, to continue chatting with her customer. I am playing just next to them with the little girl, Mireille. We amuse ourselves by chasing and then catching each other. I don't know what it is that alerts me, perhaps my mother's voice that suddenly grows quiet. I start listening, as if I were no longer breathing.

Me, September 1949, in the garden Yvetot.

I cannot replicate her story, only its content, phrases that have come down through the years until today and which spread through my childhood in an instant like a mute, heatless flame, while I continued to dance and twirl beside her, with my head down so as not to arouse suspicion.

(Here, it seems to me that the words are tearing open a crepuscular zone; they snatch me up and then it's all over.)

She says they had another daughter who died of diphtheria at age six, before the war, in Lillebonne. She describes the membranes in the throat, the suffocation. She says: *She died like a little saint*

she reports the words you said before dying: *I am going to see the Blessed Virgin and the Good Lord Jesus*

she says *my husband lost his mind* when he found you dead on returning from his job at the refineries of Port-Jérôme

she says, *it's not the same as losing your spouse*

she says of me, *she doesn't know anything, we didn't want to make her sad*

In the end, she says of you, *she was nicer than the other one*

The other one is me.

The scene of the story hasn't budged, no more than a photo would. I can see the exact position of the two women in the street in relation to each other. My mother in her white work coat, wiping her eyes from time to time with her handkerchief, the young woman in silhouette, more elegant than the usual customers, with a light-colored dress and her hair pulled back into a low chignon, her face a soft oval. (Due to memory's way of spontaneously choosing from among the multitude of beings one has met and putting them in pairs, like faces on playing cards, I now confuse her with the director of a summer camp where I worked as a monitor in

Ymare, near Rouen, in 1959; her totem name was Ant and she dressed in white and beige.)

The reality of the scene is confirmed to me, more than anything, by a sort of bodily hallucination: I *feel* myself running in close circles around the two women, I *see* the flint surface of the rue de l'École, which will not be paved until the 1980s, the bank of weeds, the fence, the fading light, as if I'd had to absorb all the scenery in the world in order to endure what was happening.

I cannot put an exact date to that summer Sunday, but I've always thought it was in August. Twenty-five years ago, while reading the journal of Cesare Pavese, I discovered he'd committed suicide in a hotel room in Turin on August 27, 1950. I immediately checked—it was a Sunday. Since then, I've imagined it was the same Sunday.

It grows more distant every year—but that is an illusion. There is no time between you and me. There are words that have never changed.

Rue de l'École, Yvetot.

Nice. I think I already knew that the word could not be applied to me, judging from the terms my parents used each day to describe me, according to my behavior: *bold, scruffy little madam, greedy, Miss Know-It-All, nasty girl, you've got the devil in you.* But their reproaches rolled off my back, so sure was I of being loved by them, the proof of which I saw in their constant concern for little me, in addition to their gifts. I was an only child and spoiled on that account, always at the top of my class without making any effort, and in short, I felt I had the right to be what I was.

Nice I was not in God's eyes either, as Father B. told me categorically when I made my first confession at seven, confessing to "wicked deeds alone and with others," which today are considered part of a normal sexual awakening but which then, according to him, would send me straight to Hell. As the headmistress of the convent school confirmed to me one day, looking me up and down with her glittering eyes, "It is possible to have perfect results in every subject and still not be pleasing to God." I showed no yearning for religion. I did not like God. I was afraid of him, though no one suspected, for I was merely withdrawn and silent when she whispered, as we knelt before the red altar light, *Pray with all your might to Good Lord Jesus*, an injunction I felt was juvenile and unworthy of the all-powerful mother that she was.

Nice also meant affectionate, sweet, "*amitieuse*" as people said in Norman dialect of dogs and little children. Distant with adults, preferring to observe and listen to them, rather than embrace them, I did not come across as such. Yet with my parents, I must have been affectionate—even more so than other children.

Sixty years later, I still stumble over the word *nice* and try to untangle the meanings it had in relation to you, and to them, though the meaning was immediately, blindingly clear in the sense that it changed my place in the family in a second. Between them and me, suddenly there was you, invisible and adored, while I was pushed aside, pushed away to make room for you. Thrust into the shadows while you soared above in the light of eternity. I was compared—me, the incomparable, the only child. Reality is an affair of words, a system of exclusions. More/Less. Or/And. Before/After. To be or not to be. Life or death.

Two words stood between my mother and me. I made her pay for them. I wrote against her. I wrote for her. I wrote in her place, that of a proud and humiliated worker. *Nicer than.* I wonder if she didn't give me permission, or even an injunction *not* to be nice. On that summer Sunday, I do not only discover my darkness, I become it with my whole being. The day of the story is the day of judgment.

At the age of twenty-two, after quarreling with my parents at the table, I write in my journal: "Why is it that I've always wanted to do evil, and yet I always suffer?"

Nothing that happens in childhood has a name. I don't know what I felt, but it wasn't sadness. More as if I'd been "swindled." But this word, which I associate with my reading of Simone de Beauvoir many years later, seems unreal, weightless, and unfit to be visited upon my being as a child. After a great deal of searching, the word that came to me, and seemed the most accurate—irrefutable—was *duped*. I'd been duped in the most colloquial sense of the word: I was mortified. I'd been living in a state of illusion. I was not unique. There was another girl, who'd sprung out of nowhere. Therefore, all the love I thought I was receiving was false.

I also think that I was angry at you for saying that you were going to see the Blessed Virgin and the Good Lord Jesus. Words that showed me the full extent of my unworthiness because I never would have uttered them. I did not want to see God. Later, as an adult, I was angry at *her* to the point of rage for having made you believe such hocus-pocus. I'm not angry anymore. I accept the idea that any sort of consolation, a prayer, a song, is worth something when a person is sinking into nothingness; and I prefer to believe that you left happy.

According to my cousin G., it was C., another cousin, who one or two years earlier had revealed your existence and your death to me. I can well imagine C. feeling very proud for having been the first to inform me of something I hadn't known before, the way I remember her being when she taught me the secrets of sex, which, because she was three years older, she knew something about. But I have no memory of it. The uniform sunshine of holiday time stretches across that moment, which is lost. Maybe I resisted believing in your existence, preferring to suppress it?

(Am I writing to resurrect you and then kill you again?)

I wonder: Maybe you're already present on that summer afternoon that must have been a year or two before the day of the story. I'm in the garden writing the tale of a little girl who is on holiday at a farm and is accidentally smothered to death beneath a *villotte*, which is how they refer in Caux country to the little piles of straw that stand in the fields after harvest. I have my father read it and he marvels at my skill in front of the café customers—to excess, I feel. I have her read it, too, but do not remember what she said.

Are you there again in the daydream that came to me repeatedly between ages five and ten? I'm lying in a cradle draped in sheer pink curtains next to J., a little refugee from Le Havre who came to Lillebonne in 1944, my favorite playmate at the public garden, with whom I was joyfully reunited once a year, in the summer, at a big meal we attended with our parents. I can see us huddled together in the cradle, like two dolls with open eyes, an image of perfect happiness. (When writing about my mother in 1986, I called it "the pink dream" but didn't put it in the book because I had my doubts about the very clichéd meaning I gave it at the time, that of a longing for the womb.)

And, naturally, you must have been there, surrounding me with your absence, somewhere in the muffled hum in which we are immersed for the first years of life. You were there in the stories told to other women at the shop, or on benches in the park where, for lack of goods and customers, she took me every afternoon during the war. But those stories left no trace in my consciousness. They have remained devoid of images and words.

The only story that has remained in my memory is the one I wasn't supposed to hear, that wasn't meant for me but was told to the elegant young woman, who must have listened with the kind of fascination people feel in relation to things they fear could happen to them too. It was the only story that was true, told in her words and with her voice, which was the voice of *authority* because she had been *there*, and because she was the stronger one in the couple (so I understood that day), capable of enduring the other's death. A story now sealed, definitive and unalterable, in which you live and die like a saint—like Thérèse de Lisieux, whose enormous photo under glass has pride of place on the bedroom wall. It is the one and only story—there will never be another—that for me inaugurates the world in which you exist as a dead girl and a saint, the one which proclaims the truth and excludes me.

When I think about it, I wonder how my mother, who must have been aware of my presence, for she had pointed at me, could have gone so far as to talk about you in front of me. The psychoanalytical explanation—which would suggest that my mother, through some ruse of her unconscious, had found a way of revealing the secret of your existence to me, and that the story was intended for me—is enticing, as ever. But the history of mentalities was unknown to her. In the fifties, adults thought of children as beings whose ears didn't count, in front of whom anything could be said without consequence, except when it came to sexual matters, which were only hinted at. I'm sure of what I am saying here because later, I heard many such accounts of death, passed from woman to woman on the train, at the hair salon, or in a kitchen over a cup of coffee, *memento mori* in which every circumstance and detail of a death are shared in an outpouring of grief. Having started to talk about you, she couldn't stop. She couldn't not go on until the end, finding in the story of your death, as told to the young mother hearing it for the first time, the consolation of a form of resurrection.

There is another story.

The photos of me as a chubby baby and a sturdy little girl are misleading. By the age of ten, when I hear the story of your death, I already have the fraught history of a delicate child, prone to accidents and unusual ailments that people enumerate in my presence, which set me apart from other children and their unexceptional cases of measles and chickenpox. I also catch these, but with me they always last longer—something between a blessing and a curse. I get off to a bad start very early on. Foot-and-mouth disease at just a few months old—an extremely rare case of transmission from cows to humans through milk in a baby bottle. Then, when I was just starting to walk, a limp discovered by a grocery store customer that left me immobilized, my legs in plaster, for half a year. A fall at age four on a bottle shard in the courtyard behind the house put a hole in my lip, of which she would say, forefinger raised, *I could have put my finger through it,* and left me with a bulging scar. In addition, myopia that grew steadily worse and teeth that were already decayed.

This inventory lacks the essential. When I was five, I almost died, and there's another story. In this one, the heroine is me. I already know it by heart on that summer Sunday when you appear in my life as a child. She, my mother, told it so many times, without hiding, in my presence— more often than my father, for it is women who keep the records of childhood—and always cheerfully, because it invariably elicited the incredulous amazement and wonder of those who heard it.

In August 1945, in the public garden of Lillebonne, I injured my knee on a rusty nail. Several days later, my abnormal fatigue, stiff neck and difficulty opening my mouth convinced them to call the doctor. He was new to the profession. After examining me, he remained silent for a moment and then said, *I hope I'm wrong, I'll go find a colleague.* It was tetanus. Neither she nor he knew what that was, they'd never heard of it. The doctors injected me with massive doses of anti-tetanus serum and said, *If her jaw doesn't unclench by evening, there's no hope.* She made me drink Lourdes water by dribbling it between my teeth, which were already clenched. My mouth opened again. The following year, in an act of thanksgiving, she went to Lourdes, traveling all night on a train with wooden seats with only a tin of sardines to eat because of the restrictions, and did the Stations of the Cross on her knees, on the mountain. She brought me back a doll who walked by herself. We named her Bernadette.

Probably because the story was told so often, the images from that time became fixed in my mind quite early, though I don't recall experiencing much fear, or anyway much less so than during the bombings. I remember the public garden full of sunshine and running to my parents because I've hurt myself while climbing on a bench with the slats torn off—these are lying in the grass. I show them the little red hole below the left knee, and they say, *It's nothing, run along and play.*

I'm on a chaise longue in the kitchen, I'm not playing and my cousin C. is with us for the holidays; after the meal she climbs up on the table and sings, *Gentil coquelicot mesdames gentil coquelicot nouveau,* and I'm jealous

I see blurred images of a commotion, people coming and going around my chaise longue

I'm in my little bed, next to theirs, and she is leaning over me

later, probably another day, my mouth fills with blood, there are people in the room and she shouts that I must be made to lie flat and that a key be put on my back to stop the hemorrhage

    I again see Bernadette, the walking doll who couldn't be sat down, she's wearing a blue dress

    The order of the two stories, mine and yours, runs counter to that of time, the march of time. It's an order in which I almost died before you did. I'm sure of this: On that Sunday in the summer of 1950, when I hear the story of your death, I'm not imagining, I'm *remembering*. I *see*, no doubt with far greater precision than now, the bedroom in Lillebonne, their bed parallel to the window, my rosewood cot beside it. I SEE YOU LYING IN MY PLACE AND IT IS ME WHO IS DYING.

    I read in a Larousse dictionary from 1949: "After onset, tetanus is most often fatal. Nevertheless cases of recovery have been cited, due to the administration of anti-tetanus serum in high, repeated doses." There is no mention of a vaccine. On the internet, I learn that it was compulsory for all children starting in 1940, but that it was not put into circulation until after 1945.

I seem to have always been convinced of the superiority of serum over Lourdes water, never mentioning the latter on the rare occasion I've recounted this episode from childhood, for example in 1964 to a medical student, in his room on the rue Bouquet, in Rouen, when he told me about his shifts at the hospital, and the tetanus patients dying in indescribable pain. Something terrible my mother told me came back to me then: *There was a time when they smothered them between two mattresses.*

One of the questions I've never asked myself is: Why weren't you given Lourdes water to drink? Or perhaps you were but it didn't work.

Serum or holy water, what does it matter? Lourdes, La Salette, Lisieux, Fátima, we lived with the idea that miracles were possible, constantly evoked by the priests and nuns at the convent school, and in the brochures sold at the church, which at the time included *Le Pèlerin* and *La Croix*. Even "little Marie," one of the children of "Brigitte"—herself a paragon of womanhood and the main character of the eponymous best-selling serial—was cured of her handicap with water from the grotto.

Reality does not penetrate the beliefs of childhood. In 1950, I lived with a belief in miracles. Maybe I still do. The only thing that matters is what the first story—about my impending death and my resurrection—did to the second one—about your death and my unworthiness. How they came together. The active truths they constructed. Because I had to come to terms with this mysterious contradiction—you, the good girl, the little saint, were not saved, and I, the demon, survived. Not only survived, was miraculously saved.

So you had to die at six for me to come into the world and be saved.

Pride and guilt at having, for some indecipherable reason, been chosen for survival. Maybe more pride at my survival than guilt. But chosen to do what? When I was twenty, after a voyage through hell with bulimia and the drying of my menstrual blood, an answer came: to write. In my room at my parents' home, I pinned up this sentence by Claudel, carefully copied onto a big sheet of paper, the edges burnt with a lighter, like a pact with Satan: "Yes, I believe that I did not come into the world for nothing and that there is something in me that the world cannot do without."

I do not write because you died. You died so I would write; that makes a big difference.

I have only six photos of you, all of which were given to me by cousins, some after my mother's burial, others very recently. I'd only known of two, which my mother kept in a drawer in her wardrobe and which disappeared around 1980, probably thrown away in one of the outbursts of destructive rage that were early signs of Alzheimer's.

In these photos, apart from the one of you as a baby, you must be between four and six. No doubt they were taken with the camera they said they'd won at a fair before the war, and which they kept until the end of the fifties. I used it often. You almost always have your head down and are grimacing, or shielding your eyes with your arm, as if the light hurts you—as if it were unbearable. In a recent letter, my cousin G., who also noticed this, remarked: "She doesn't look as if she likes herself much."

I am violently disturbed by this remark. Were you happy? I've never asked myself the question, as if it were an absurd, outrageous thing to ask about a little dead girl. As if their pain at losing you and their missing your niceness—proof of their love—guaranteed your happiness. If there is truth to the belief that happiness comes of being loved, you must have been happy—you couldn't have been otherwise. Saints are happy. But maybe you weren't.

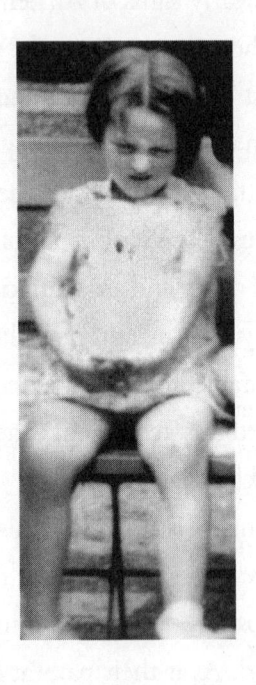

My sister, 1937.

Horror and guilt to catch myself thinking the unbidden thought: You were obviously not cut out for life, your death was programmed into the computer of the universe and you were sent to earth, as Bossuet writes, "to be a mere number." Shame to feel the old belief return, that you had to die, be sacrificed so that I could be born.

There was no predestination. Just a diphtheria epidemic and the fact that you weren't vaccinated. According to Wikipedia, the vaccine was made compulsory on November 25, 1938. You died seven months before.

Two daughters, one dead and one who almost died. As long as she lived, she who was life in all its exuberance seemed to me a bringer of death. Attracted to and attracting death. Until I was fourteen or fifteen, in some muddled way I believed that she would let me die, as she had you. Or that she'd let herself die on purpose, as part of a general punishment of everyone, including my father, implied by the remark she flung at us on days of great anger, *You'll see how it is when I'm gone* (but wasn't this more a threat to leave us to go live somewhere else?). Neighbors came to her for help with the dying, and for washing and laying out the dead. She would rush off and return in a peculiar state in which I thought I discerned a kind of satisfaction. She said of a young girl who died of tuberculosis, *With the sheet draped around her head, she looked like Saint Thérèse de Lisieux.* When I had to have an operation on my hip at forty-five, I thought I wouldn't waken from the anesthesia, that I'd die before her—so she would *bury us all*, you, then my father and then me.

In a drawing by Reiser, a man is seen from the back leading a child by the hand over a long narrow bridge, without railings, across an abyss.

Behind them, on the right, the bridge has a strip cut out of it, with empty space beyond. Ahead of them, to the left, the side the child is walking on, there's an identical gap. We can tell by the footprints—those of the adult, framed by those of *two* children, one on either side—that the father has already let a first child drop into the void, is about to do the same with the second and then calmly proceed alone to the other side of the bridge. The title of the drawing is *The Bridge of Lost Children*.

But the facts belie the myth. She bundled me up to excess in the winter, sent my father for the doctor at the slightest hint of a cold, took me to see specialists in Rouen, and paid for dental work whose cost was beyond their means. She bought calf's liver and red meat just for me, though her remark, "You're costing us an arm and a leg," sounded like a reproach for my fragility. I felt guilty for coughing and "always having something wrong with me." My survival cost them dearly.

Naturally, I adored her. People said she was a beautiful woman and that I "took after her." I prided myself on being like her. And sometimes I hated her and shook my fist at the wardrobe mirror, wishing she would die. Writing to you means talking nonstop about her, the keeper of the story, the voice of judgment, with whom the fighting never ceased, except at the end, when she was in such misery, so lost in her madness, and I didn't want her to die.

Between her and me it's a question of words.

I've been unable from the start to write *our mother*, or *our parents*—to add you to the trio of my childhood. There is no possessive we can share.

(Is this a way of excluding you, of responding in kind to my being excluded from the story told on that summer Sunday?)

From one—significant—perspective, that of time, we were raised by different parents.

When you were born in 1932, they were young, scarcely four years married, workers with ambitions who had taken on debt the year before to set up a business in the Vallée, the spinning mill district of Lillebonne. He continued to work outside the business, on a construction site in Hode and then at the refineries in Port-Jérôme. The hopes awakened by the Front Populaire bubbled inside and around them. The stories of those years of living hand-to-mouth, of evenings spent working in their café until three in the morning, always ended with "but we were young then."

In an undated photo from before the war, he holds her by the shoulders, smiling. She wears a dress with big polka dots and a pale lace collar. A thick lock of hair falls over her eyes. She still resembles the sleek and rebellious young bride of 1928. I never saw her in that dress or with that hairstyle. I did not know the woman of that time, of your time.

At the beginning of mine, in photos in which I also appear, probably from the spring of 1945, although they are smiling there is no longer anything youthful or carefree about them, but something broken. Their features are marked, heavy-looking. She's in a striped dress that I saw her wear for a long time. Her hair is swept up in a roll. They have lived through the Exodus, the Occupation, the bombings. They have lived through your death. They are parents who have lost a child.

You are there between them, invisible. Their pain.

They must have used the expression "when you grow up," listing the things you'd learn to do—read, ride a bicycle, walk to school by yourself—and said, "next year," "this summer," "soon." One evening, instead of a future there was only emptiness. They said the same words again, to me. I was six, seven, ten; I'd overtaken you. There was no longer any way for them to compare. Obscurely, I believed she was angry with me for ceasing to be a child, "becoming a young woman," as she said, on the day of my first period, with disproportionate embarrassment, verging on distress, as she handed me a sanitary towel.

The story that I overheard was the first and last I ever heard. Neither of them ever talked to me about you.

I don't know when it was that they hid your photos in the wardrobe, and the family record book in a rusty strongbox in the attic, where I read it one day—I was at least eighteen—when the box was left open. Every week they took turns cycling to the cemetery with flowers from the garden. Sometimes one would discreetly ask the other, *Have you been to the cemetery?* Long before they knew they'd be going back there, seven years later, in 1945, it was in Yvetot—where almost all the members of the two families lived—that they'd wanted you to be buried, and not in Lillebonne, probably so that people would go often to visit your grave.

I never heard them say your name. I learned it from my cousin C. As an adolescent, I thought it seemed old-fashioned, almost ridiculous. None of the girls at school had that name. Even now, on hearing it, I feel uneasy, vaguely repelled. I hardly ever say it, as if to do so were forbidden. Ginette.

They never said anything about the things that had belonged to you and they had kept.

They had me sleep in your rosewood cot until I was about seven. After that, they bought me a corner unit, a single bed with shelving, and the cot was dismantled, the four panels, wooden frame, and metal bedsprings put away in the attic, reassembled from time to time for a visiting child to sleep in. When my mother came to live with us in Annecy, she brought it with her other furniture. I stored it in the basement, from where some moving men mistakenly transported it to my parents'-in-law in Charente, who, without telling me, hastily disposed of it, as they told me with an offhand laugh in the summer of 1971.

Until the start of secondary school, they made me go to class with the brown Morocco leather briefcase that you had started school with. No one else but me had one like it, and it was awkward to use. When the bag was opened, both compartments had to be flipped over in one sharp movement, otherwise the pencil case and notebooks would tumble out and scatter. Because I'd always seen it around the house, I thought it had been bought for me, years in advance of my first day of school. I must have been over twenty when I realized that the briefcase—which she always kept for storing papers in—was yours.

I find this written in my journal of August 1992: "As a child—is this the origin of writing?—I always thought I was the double of another girl living in another place. That I wasn't really living, either, and that this life was 'writing,' a fiction about another girl. This absence of being, or fictional being, needs to be explored further."

Perhaps this is the purpose of this fake letter; for the only real letters are ones that are written to the living.

Only today do I ask myself the question, so simple yet it never occurred to me before: Why did I never, at any time, ask them about you, even as an adult and a mother myself? Why did I never tell them that I knew? At a certain point, all that is revealed by a delay in asking a question, whether private or collective, is the very impossibility of doing so. In the fifties, an implicit rule forbade us from asking our parents, or adults in general, about things they didn't want us to know but that we knew. On that Sunday in the summer of my tenth birthday, I was given both the story and the law of silence. I wasn't supposed to ask them anything because they didn't want me finding out about you. I was supposed to comply with their desire for me not to know about you. It seems to me that breaking that law (but I did not even imagine doing so) would have been tantamount to uttering obscenities in front of them, or doing something even worse—bringing on a kind of cataclysm and an unusual punishment that I associate here with the phrase of Kafka's father to his son, who relates it in his "Letter to His Father," and which I immediately copied down the first time I read it, at the age of twenty-two, on my bed in the university halls of residence: *I will tear you apart like a fish.*

I remember the terror I felt at age sixteen, while visiting my aunt Marie-Louise, who, in her usual Sunday state of drunkenness, forgot what she wasn't supposed to talk about and said, *That's your sister*, pointing to you in a photo that I didn't even look at in my haste to move on to the next one, panic-stricken at the thought that the two of them, standing nearby, had heard what she'd said and therefore learned that I knew their secret.

We maintained the pretense beyond a point anyone would have believed possible.

In June 1967, my father's coffin was lowered into the fresh grave dug next to yours, which she and I pretended not to see. The following summer, while on holiday at her house, I went to lay flowers from the garden on my father's grave. I didn't put any on yours, since she hadn't told me anything. Even the place where you are buried was never named.

At some point they must have realized (though when that was, and what gave me away I will never know) that I knew about you. It had grown much too late to break the silence, the secret was too old. It had become too complicated for them to lift the ban. It seems to me that I lived quite well with the way things were. Children live better than one might think with secrets, with things they believe must not be said.

I think that silence suited both them and me. It protected me. It spared me the weight of veneration that surrounded certain children in the family who had died, at the cost of unintended cruelty toward living children that revolted me every time I witnessed it. The mother of my cousin C. never ceased to praise her sister Monique, who died at three, and who, according to their mother, *would have been a beauty*. My parents had denied themselves the possibility of holding you up as a model child, of saying to my face, *She was nicer than you.*

I didn't want them to talk to me about you. Maybe I hoped that if they didn't, they'd forget you over time. I see the confirmation of this hypothesis in the memory of a deep, inexplicable disquiet I felt as an adult every time I had to admit the obvious: Your presence inside them was indestructible.

In 1983, to the doctor testing her fleeing memory in my presence, amidst a series of crazy answers, my mother says, *I had two daughters*—the only answer that is true. She does not remember the year of her own birth. Instead, she gives the year of your death, 1938.

In 1965, my husband and I come to visit from Bordeaux with our firstborn of six months, whom my parents have not yet seen. When we get out of the car, he is there, overwhelmed with joy to see his grandson at last, and exclaims, *The little girl has arrived!* I wish I hadn't heard that slip of the tongue, whose full significance I now appreciate, including its beauty. It discouraged me, cast a shadow over me. Perhaps it also made my skin crawl. I didn't want you to be resurrected in my child, resurrected through my body.

(Is it not, in some way, your resurrection, purged of all bonds of blood and body, that I am seeking through this letter?)

With their silence, they were also protecting themselves. Protecting you, putting you beyond the reach of my curiosity, which would have torn them apart. They kept you to themselves, inside themselves, as if in a tabernacle to which I was forbidden access. You were their sacred object. The thing that united them more surely than all the rest—more than their never-ending arguments and scenes. In June 1952, he dragged her to the cellar, he wanted to kill her. I intervened. I don't know whether it was because of me or because of you that he didn't. I remember thinking just after, *He's crazy like he was when she died*, and, weeping, I asked her, "Has he ever been like that before?" hoping she'd say yes. She didn't answer.

I don't blame them for anything. The parents of a dead child don't know what their pain does to the one who is living.

One after the other, they took to their graves the living memory of you and of all that was lost in April 1938. Your first steps, your games, the things you feared and hated as a child, your first day of school—all that prehistory of you, made dreadful by your death, and which, conversely, when it came to me, they repeated to their heart's content. My storied childhood, full of anecdotes, has little correspondence with the pure emptiness of yours.

I have never ascribed the slightest flaw to you, the slightest childish foolishness or the kinds of acts for which I was punished when I was the same age as you, as on that day when I treacherously cut a curl from my cousin C.'s hair while she was reading. You are the very impossibility of sin and punishment. You have none of the traits of a real child. Like the saints, you had no childhood. I've never imagined you as real.

But why, when there was still time, did I never question the aunts and uncles who knew you? Or Denise, the cousin four or five years older than you, who appears with you in photos, and whom I didn't know because of a falling out between my mother and hers before the war; Denise who died last year without my ever having tried to meet her. So I didn't want to know. I wanted to keep you just as you were when I received you at age ten. Dead and pure. A myth.

Valliquerville (near Yvetot), 1935. Standing left, my father; an unknown woman; my grandfather; Uncle Henri, my father's brother; Cécile, his wife; in front, Jean, Uncle Henri's son; my sister Ginette; an unknown child.

I remember a photo of you that remained for a long time on the mantel of the unused fireplace in my parents' bedroom, beside two statues of the Virgin, one brought back from the Lourdes trip after my recovery, coated with a yellow paint that made it glow in the dark, the other one older and made of alabaster, with a strange ear of wheat in Mary's arms. It was a retouched art photo, under glass and in a metal stand, showing just your head emerging from a snowy, bluish background, with glossy wings of black hair, *à la* Louise Brooks, your mouth dark as if rouged, your skin white, and as I recall, lightly tinted pink in the cheeks.

It is this lost photo that I'd have liked to include among these pages, the one of you as a saint that lives in my imagination. Not any of the photos in my possession. The very idea of displaying one of those makes my blood run cold, like a sacrilege.

Before starting this letter, I was in a state of calm—now shattered—in relation to you. As I write, I seem more and more to be moving through a muddy terrain with no one in it, as in dreams—of having, between each word, to navigate a space filled with indistinct matter. I feel I have no language for you, none with which to speak of you, as if I cannot talk about you except through the mode of negation, of continuous nonbeing. You are outside the language of feelings and emotions. You are the anti-language.

I cannot tell a story about you. I've no memory of you other than a scene I imagined the summer I was ten, in which the dead girl and the girl who was saved merge with each other. I have nothing from which to make you exist, apart from the frozen images in photos that lack voice and animation because the techniques for preserving these things were not yet in general use. Just as there are people who have died without being photographed, you are one of those who died without being captured on audio or video.

You have no existence except through the mark you left on mine. Writing to you is nothing more than walking in circles inside your absence, marking out the legacy of absence. You are an empty form, impossible to fill with writing.

I could not, or would not (for the self of the past, it comes down to the same thing) enter their pain. It predated me, it was alien. It excluded me.

I didn't like to guess its presence from the tremulous, desperate way she sang the hymn to the Virgin in processions, *I'll see her there one day*, with its refrain, *In Heaven, in Heaven*, that pushed voices to the breaking point—or in his abrupt bouts of silence, his air of suddenly thinking of something else, and his perpetual fear, at the slightest delay on my part in getting home from school because of a film or a bike ride, that *something had happened to me,* to which I would retort with pride and bad faith, *What do you want to happen to me?*

But for a long time, I heard their pain without identifying it; I knew it without knowing where it came from

in the hoarse lament of the mother cat whose kittens had been snatched from her and buried alive, in peasant fashion—kittens that one day I decided to dig up straightaway, dragging a cousin into the scheme (she still remembers it), receiving from the hand of he who'd done the burying the first and last slap he ever gave me

in the Gospel of Matthew, the words of the prophet Jeremiah, *Rachel weeping for her children in the desert and refusing to be consoled because they are no more*

in *la raison perdue* of Du Périer to whom Malherbe addressed an imbecilic, priggish *Consolation* on the death of M. Du Périer's daughter that we had to learn by heart at thirteen years of age

in the only verse of André Chénier's that I remember, *Myrto, the young Tarentine bride, once lived*

I wasn't living in their pain, I was living in your absence.

It was only on receiving a letter, thirteen years ago, from Francis G., a neighbor from Lillebonne who was just a little boy at the time of your death, that I grew closer to their pain for the first time: "Everyone in the Vallée, and many others too, remember your parents and your sister Ginette, who died of diphtheria at the age of six. My cousins (Yvette and Jacqueline H.) told me that for more than eight days, customers didn't dare go to the grocery shop, for it was so sad to see your parents' grief. Perhaps they were also afraid of that terrible illness." It's as if I needed the words of people who were still alive and had witnessed the event for me to feel the reality of my parents' suffering.

If I run through the list of emotions, I can't find any that I felt for you in childhood, or beyond. Not hatred, which is futile, because you're dead, or tenderness—none of the kind of thing that one human being, close or distant, awakens in another. It was a blankness of feeling. A neutral, or at most, defensive feeling, if ever I suspected your unnamed presence in their allusions to "the grave."

Or else an obscure fear. That you would retaliate.

I don't remember thinking of you. The ceaseless novelty of the knowledge presented to my appetite and pride—Latin! algebra!—and imaginary constructions around love and sex kept me occupied. What sort of weight could the insubstantial image of a little girl who died before the war have in the present life of an adolescent girl, who didn't even want to remember the child she had been and was dreaming of the future? Compared to all the things that happen, whether fortunate (getting your period, falling in love, reading *A Woman's Life* by Guy de Maupassant or *The Flowers of Evil* by Charles Baudelaire) or unfortunate (that Sunday in 1952), or that do not happen at all in the torpid boredom of summer holidays in Yvetot but would happen one day—promised by the cheerful cold of school mornings, love songs and the rapt look of girl students getting off the train from Rouen on Saturdays—your death could not have counted for much.

You were six years old forever, while I was moving forward in the world, with—I found this definition in a poem by Éluard at twenty—my "enduring desire to endure." The only thing that happened to you was death.

I wanted to live. I was afraid of disease, of cancer. The summer I was thirteen and started to limp again, a little, I didn't say anything but stuffed paper in the heel of my shoe so it wouldn't show, lest I be put in a cast again and sent to Berck-Plage. Perhaps I drew my strength from you, from your death and my survival, which I considered to be a miracle. Perhaps you gave me extra energy, a lust for life, the same as what the students at the Saint-Hilaire-du-Touvet sanatorium felt in the sixties, haunted as they were, despite the discovery of antibiotics, by the deaths from tuberculosis that were still so recent, and (was it a coincidence?) I would choose to marry one of those students, who had titled his diary "Agony."

I was aware of my advantages as an only

child, a child born after the death of another, the pampered object of a worried solicitude. He wanted me above all to be happy, she wanted me to *be a good person*, and, within the family and in our working-class neighborhood, their desires added up to an enviable existence for me—that of a privileged girl who was never sent to fetch the bread and who said "I don't serve" to customers, on the grounds that she was continuing her education. You were their sorrow. I knew I was their hope, the source of complications, of events, from the First Communion to the *bac*, their success. I was their future.

Sometimes I calculated how old you would have been, approximately, because for a long time I didn't know the exact year of your birth, with your eight- or ten-years' seniority. The age gap was infinite. I had to picture you as a grown-up girl, like those who used to come around the shop and considered me an unimportant little kid. I didn't miss having a sister like these older girls who would have dominated me with her superior age, her breasts, her knowledge and her rights. With you I would not have shared anything. The idea of a younger, or even a baby sister, like a living doll, appealed to me more.

But you and I were fated to be only children. Their desire to have just one child, which they made very clear (*we couldn't do for two what we are doing for one*), meant it was either you or me, but not both.

It took almost thirty years and the writing of *A Man's Place* for me to put together these two facts that had always remained separate in my mind—your death, and their having only one child, for economic reasons—and for it to hit me: I was born because you died, and I replaced you.

I cannot avoid this question: If I hadn't wanted to stay as close as possible to reality in the writing of that book, *A Man's Place*, would you have come back up from the darkness inside me, where I'd been keeping you for all those years? Is it from my writing that you have been reborn, from my descent with every book into something I can't know ahead of time, as now, when I feel as if I'm pulling back curtains that continue to multiply in an endless corridor?

Or would the psychoanalytical spirit of the times not have led me to you anyway, without my knowing it, by enjoining me to lift the backdrop of my writing and flush out the phantom who, it seems, is always lurking there, in relation to whom the writer is nothing but a puppet? And, if that is so, should I not, in writing this letter, consider you a creation of psychoanalysis and its relentless struggle to ensure, in a return to primitivism, that we never escape the dead?

The "you" is a trap. There's something suffocating about it. Between us, it creates an imaginary closeness that smacks of grievance—intimacy breeds reproach. It has a subtle way of making you the cause of my being, reducing the whole of my existence to your death.

For the temptation is great to want to trace some of my own patterns back to you, based on a rigorous weighing up of happiness and pain, such as my fear that every moment of pleasure will be followed by sorrow, and every success by an unknown punishment. Or—to reverse this principle of equivalence—the form of calculation I've applied at every level but the sexual since adolescence: suffering in order to obtain happiness or success, which prompted me to take the baccalaureate exam in an out-of-fashion skirt with pleats to gain acceptance, and to stoically endure torment at the dentist's in the hope that it would bring back a lover who had left. But this kind of sacrifice that "pays off" is more likely to be a selfish misdirection of the Christian obligation to offer up our suffering to save the souls of sinners.

Do you exist in me as an invention of the Christian religion? Such as the *real presence* of the host—the host which on the day of my solemn communion, I tore to pieces with the tip of my tongue because it had stuck to the roof of my mouth; and thereafter I believed I was in a state of mortal sin, my state of darkness growing more intense with every month due to my terror of confessing my sin, and thus sinking more and more deeply, from one bad communion to the next into the certainty that I was damned.

All I'm doing here is chasing after a shadow.

Rather than within, perhaps I should be looking for you outside myself in those girls I'd have liked to have been, pupils in the years ahead of me in school. Even just to write their names here—Madeleine Tourmente, Françoise Renout, Janine Belleville—is to once again become the schoolgirl in the blue smock of nine or ten or eleven years old, who searched the schoolyard for those mysterious goddesses from whom I did not expect the slightest glance, to say nothing of a word. It was enough just to see them.

Or—more reliably—I should look for you in scenes from novels, films, and paintings, never forgotten, that have troubled me for years without my knowing why. That is probably where I should be looking for you—in that private repertoire of the imagination, illegible to others, and through the kind of work that no one else can claim to do on our behalf. I already know that it's you in *Jane Eyre*, slipped into the character of wise and pious Helen Burns, Jane's older friend at the sinister Lowood School—Helen, consumed by tuberculosis, whom Jane, miraculously unscathed by the typhus fever that is wiping out the boarders, goes to see one evening in the infirmary. Helen asks her to come lie next to her in bed.

"You came to bid me good-bye, then: you are just in time probably."

"Are you going somewhere, Helen? Are you going home?"

"Yes; to my long home—my last home."

"No, no, Helen!"

. . .

"But where are you going to, Helen? Can you see? Do you know?"

"I believe; I have faith: I am going to God."

"Where is God? What is God?"

In the morning, they come to untangle Jane from Helen—Jane, asleep with her arm around Helen, who is dead.

Le Havre, 1937. My father; to his right, my cousin Denise; in front, my sister Ginette.

Before me is a photo that my cousin C. sent me about twenty years ago. There are three of you standing on the sidewalk at the corner of two streets. My father, tall and smiling in a dark, double-breasted suit, very dressed up, holding a hat in his hand (I only ever knew him to wear berets). Beside him, a girl in a long white First Communion dress, his niece Denise. Only her face can be seen, framed by the headpiece to which the veil is attached, and her ankles. In front of her is a little dark-haired girl whose head comes up to her chest. That is you. You too are all in white—a short-sleeved dress, ankle socks and T-strap shoes. Your hair, parted in the middle, squared off just below your ears, with a pin-on bow on the left side, forms a dark and strangely perfect arc around your very high rounded forehead. You look at the camera unsmiling, with a look of gravity on your face. Your mouth appears dark red, a striking detail along with the gesture you are making, the fingers of both hands spread wide apart and pressed together at the tips. Because of the white-against-white of the two dresses you seem to merge into the other girl, the communicant whose veil covers your upper arms. On the wall behind the group is a poster with large letters, reading *The High Cost of Living—Food Reform for the Working Class—Wage Increases—Paid Holidays—The Forty-Hour Week*. A large building can be seen in the distance—a sign on its side reads "La Méditerranée"—with several indistinct forms moving toward it. The formal clothing of the group of three contrasts with the vague desolation of the setting, which is urban and semi-industrial. The photo was taken in Le Havre in 1937. You are five years old. You have one year left to live.

I look at your serious expression, your fingers that are playfully spread, your frail legs. In the photo, you're no longer the evil shadow from my childhood, you're no longer the saint. You're a little girl who was abruptly removed from time in the middle of a diphtheria epidemic, torn from the face of the earth, which, at that moment, on that day, a holiday, had the shape and substance of a stretch of sidewalk bordered with cement in a working-class district of Le Havre.

I am overwhelmed by the expanse of my life, infinitely larger than yours. The things that are behind me are innumerable, things seen and heard, learned and forgotten—women and men I've met, streets, mornings and evenings. I feel overwhelmed by the profusion of images.

Very distant, but so clear, are the very first ones of Lillebonne:

the café, with the billiard table, the marble-topped tables in parallel rows, the silhouettes of customers, indistinct except for those of a couple sitting at a table, the Foldrains; the wife only had two or three teeth left

the kitchen, separated from the grocery shop by a door with a window, opening onto the little cobblestoned courtyard

the dining room at the top of the stairs, with black and orange celluloid flowers in a bowl on the table

Poupette the dog, a short-haired and perpetually shivering female who killed the rats brought in by the river

the brown hulk of the Desgenétais spinning mills with their huge iron-ringed chimneys

the mill and its wheel tinged with green

I put these images in my books. So strange

to think that they were images from your life too. Even stranger to realize that you and I exist together in people's memories, as this passage from a letter of 1997 from Francis G. attests: "My cousin Yvette told me that when the weather was fine, she'd take your sister Ginette for a walk in her stroller along the road to La Trinité-du-Mont. As for Jacqueline, she remembers holding you in her arms when you were a tiny baby, that your little legs were both in plaster casts, and that Mme Duchesne told her to be especially careful."

I see the blurred forms of people from Lillebonne who knew you, whose names buzzed around you, Meurget, Bordeaux, Vincent, Eude, Tranchant, Abbé Leclerc and the owners of the mill, the Bosches, who had a monkey for a pet. I can hear the names of streets and places that you heard too, places to which I've never returned since 1945, rue Césarine and rue Goubertmoulin, La Frénaye, Le Becquet.

I remember the grandparents, the uncles and aunts, the cousins who remembered you. I've written about them.

We both emerged into consciousness in the same world. Heat and cold, hunger and thirst, food, the day's weather, everything in existence was conveyed to us with the same voices, the same gestures and the same language, the French that I will be told at school is not the "right" one.

We were rocked to sleep with the same songs. His was *Quand tu seras dans la purée reviens vers moi*, hers *Le temps des cerises* and a sad song, *C'est l'amour qui flotte dans l'air à la ronde, c'est l'amour qui console le pauvre monde*.

We were born from the same body. I've never really wanted to think about this.

I can see myself in the kitchen, in Lillebonne. It's the evening, after supper, and the shop is closed. I'm sitting in her lap, snuggled up against her chest, and she's singing, *Sur le pont du Nord*, he is sitting opposite

on a gray Sunday in Yvetot, we're going for a walk and they're holding my hands; I watch their shoes move along the stony road, and mine next to them, so little.

In these images, I never picture you instead of me. I cannot see you in the places where I see myself with them.

I can't put you in the places where I've been, replace my existence with yours. There is death and there is life. You or me. In order for me to be, I had to deny you.

In 2003, in my journal, picturing the scene of the story, I wrote: "I'm not *nice* like her, I'm excluded. So I will not be cut out for love, but for solitude and intelligence."

Several years ago, I stopped in Lillebonne, the Vallée district. On rue de la Tannerie, I saw the outside of the café-grocery where both of us were born and learned it had been a private home since the 1970s. The façade, roughcast in an aggressive white that stood out against the gray of its neighbors, had been completely redone—the door to the shop had been made into a window and all signs of the former business erased. I hadn't wanted to see the inside. While knowing that reality does not preserve itself and must be continually consolidated, repainted and reupholstered, I dreaded the kind of injury inflicted on memory by other people's furniture and renovations.

Last summer, before I even thought of writing this letter, I started to feel the desire to enter the house the next time, a desire that grew more and more pressing with each new difficulty I encountered in reaching the current

Rue de la Tannerie, Lillebonne.

occupants, and then in overcoming their legitimate but to me unbearable reluctance to open their door to me. It was as if I were expecting it to bring some kind of revelation, whose purpose I could not imagine—for writing, maybe, but that was secondary.

After an exchange of letters and emails, the owners, a couple in their fifties, agreed to let me enter the house last April. It was the first time I'd been inside since 1945.

On the ground floor, everything seemed to have been transformed, the partitions knocked down to form a single room. I only recognized the very low ceiling—I could almost touch it by stretching my arm up—and the small courtyard by the river. The toilets, laundry room, and rabbit hutches had disappeared. Upstairs, it seemed to me that a partition had been added to create a narrow hallway—absent, in my recollection—between the two bedrooms on the street side and the other two that faced the courtyard. The first one on the right was the couple's, as it had once been my parents' room. The bed stood in the same place as before, parallel to the window. Everything corresponded on a smaller scale to what I'd remembered. No doubt if I'd been brought to the room blindfolded, I wouldn't have been able to say where I was, but as it happened, I could have no doubt that it was the very same room (a fact guaranteed by the presence of a window on the river side, as in the image I'd always retained) as the one of 1945.

I looked at the bed and tried to replace it with that of my parents, to picture the little rosewood cot beside it. I had no real thoughts, only: "It's there." I experienced a kind of overwhelming sensation, astonishment and obscure contentment at being there, in that exact place in the world, between those walls, near that window—at being the gaze that contemplates the room where everything began, for one girl and then the other. Where it was all decided. The room of life and death, bathed in light that late afternoon. The place where the enigma of chance played out.

Here, I sometimes see the light-filled room of last April, I feel the disconcerting presence of the owner beside me, I feel the heat; sometimes I'm in the other room, twilit, indistinct—a little shadow lying between the sides of my cot. The first room, where I never experienced anything, will disappear of its own accord in a relatively short time, that's how it always goes, in my experience—the furniture, the color of the bedspread already forgotten. The other room is indestructible.

Peter Pan fled through the open window after seeing his parents leaning over his cradle. One day he returns and finds the window closed. There is another child in the cradle. He flees again. He will never grow up. In some versions, he comes into houses looking for children who are about to die. You probably didn't know this version of the story. I didn't either until my ninth-grade English class. I never liked it.

On November 7, 1945, three weeks after their return to Yvetot, they bought a plot in the cemetery, right next to you. He was put there first, in 1967, and she nineteen years later. I will not be buried in Normandy next to you. I never wanted or imagined that. The other girl is me, the one who fled, who went far away from them to another place.

In a few days I'll go visit the graves, as I usually do on All Saints' Day. I don't know if I'll have anything to say to you this time, or whether going is even worth it. Whether I'll feel ashamed or proud of having written this letter. Why I started it in the first place remains a mystery.

Perhaps I wanted to repay an imaginary debt by giving you, in turn, the existence your death gave me. Or to make you live and die again, so I could call it quits with you, get out from under your shadow. Get away from you.

Fight against the long, long life of the dead.

Obviously, this letter isn't meant for you, and you won't be reading it. It is others who'll receive it, readers who, when I'm writing, are as invisible as you. Yet a trace of magical thinking in me wants it to reach you, in some inconceivable, analogical way, just as, one summer Sunday long ago that may have been the day when Pavese committed suicide in a hotel room in Turin, I learned of your existence through a story that wasn't meant for me.

October 2010

WORKS BY ANNIE ERNAUX

In order of publication in English, followed by the dates of original publication in French.

Cleaned Out, 1974

A Woman's Story, 1987

A Man's Place, 1983

Simple Passion, 1991

A Frozen Woman, 1981

Exteriors, 1993

Shame, 1997

"I Remain in Darkness," 1997

Happening, 2000

The Possession, 2002

Things Seen, 2000

The Years, 2008

A Girl's Story, 2016

Getting Lost, 2001

Do What They Say or Else, 1977

Look at the Lights, My Love, 2014

I Will Write to Avenge My People: The Nobel Lecture, 2023

The Young Man, 2022

The Use of Photography, 2005

The Other Girl, 2011